At the Medical Room

Written by Helen Dineen

Illustrated by Lucy Makuc

Collins

Crash! Travis trips on a plastic block.

Ow! What a bump! What must Travis do now?

Travis is hurt, so he must get help.

Travis limps to the medical room.
Fred helps.

Miss Smith is glad to help Travis.

pen

chair

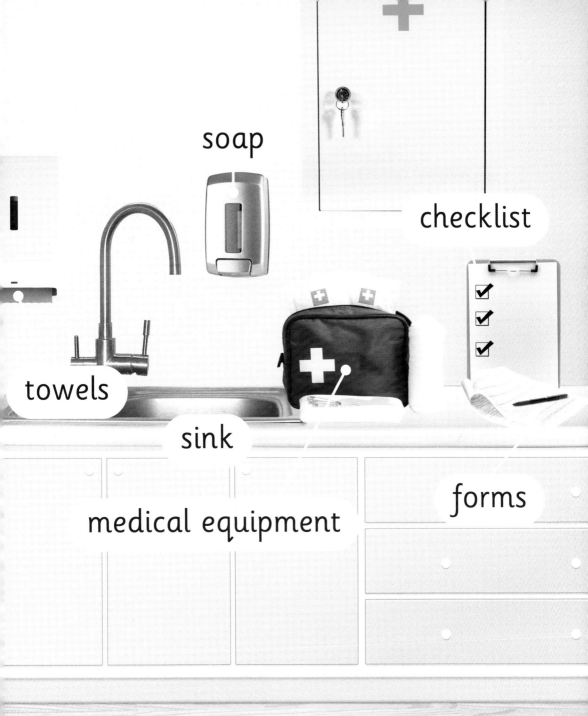

soap

checklist

towels

sink

medical equipment

forms

Miss Smith tells Travis to rest.

She checks the cut for grit and mud.

Greg has hurt his hand. Zainab has a splinter.

Astrid feels sick and has spots.
Grandad collects her.

Miss Smith fills in a sheet at her desk.

The children feel better. They all have stickers.

Help

After reading

Letters and Sounds: Phase 4

Word count: 100

Focus on adjacent consonants with short vowel phonemes, e.g. *trips*

Common exception words: to, the, do, what, so, he, she, have, they, all

Curriculum links (EYFS): Understanding the world

Curriculum links: (National Curriculum, Year 1) Animals, including humans

Early learning goals: Reading: read and understand simple sentences; use phonic knowledge to decode regular words and read them aloud accurately; read some common irregular words; demonstrate understanding when talking with others about what they have read.

National Curriculum learning objectives: Reading/word reading: read accurately by blending sounds in unfamiliar words containing GPCs that have been taught; Reading/comprehension: understand both the books they can already read accurately and fluently and those they listen to by checking that the text makes sense to them as they read, and correcting inaccurate reading

Developing fluency

- Take turns with your child to read a page, checking that your child pauses at commas, and adjusts their expression to suit the sentences that have exclamation and question marks.

Phonic practice

- Take turns to point to a word with adjacent consonants for the other to sound out and blend. (e.g. **limps**, **glad**) Occasionally pick a word with more than one syllable (e.g. **equipment**, **checklist**).
- When it is your turn to read, occasionally make an error sounding out the adjacent consonants, and say: I'm not sure I got that right. Work together to read it correctly.

Extending vocabulary

- Ask your child to think of a word or phrase (synonym) that means the same as the following:
  o **equipment** (e.g. *tools, instruments*)
  o **hurt** (e.g. *injured, cut*)
  o **sick** (e.g. *poorly, ill, unwell*)